Disney's

WINNIE the POOH'S
A to Zzzz

Library of Congress Catalog Card Number: 91-73812
ISBN: 1-56282-015-X

Disney's
WINNIE the POOH'S
A to Zzzz

BY Don Ferguson • ILLUSTRATED BY Bill Langley and Diana Wakeman

Disney
PRESS

NEW YORK

A

IS

FOR

ACORN

From atop an oak tree
In the Hundred-Acre Wood
A little acorn fell
Right where Pooh Bear stood.

B

IS

FOR

BEARS

Some bears growl,
Some bears snort,
But Pooh Bear is
The humming sort.

C

IS

FOR

CARROTS

Carrots are so
Good to munch,
Rabbit grows them
By the bunch.

D

IS

FOR

DOOR

In spring, Pooh's door
Is open wide
To let the sunshine
Come inside.

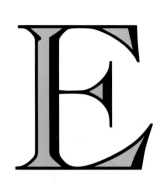 IS
FOR
EEYORE

Eeyore's gray,
Although it's true,
He's frequently
A little blue.

F

IS

FOR

FOOTPRINTS

Our footprints always follow us
On days when it's been snowing.
They always show us where we've been,
But never where we're going.

G

IS

FOR

GOPHER

"Hello!" says Gopher
To Winnie the Pooh.
"I've just come up
To visit with you!"

H

IS

FOR

HONEY

"My favorite snack,"
Says Winnie the Pooh,
"Is one jar of honey…
Or possibly two!"

HONEY

I

IS

FOR

ICE SKATES

Though others give
Him funny glances,
On ice skates Pooh Bear
Takes no chances.

J

IS

FOR

JUMP

Rum-tee-tiddle-tum
Tiddle-tum-too,
When Kanga jumps,
So does Roo.

K

IS

FOR

KITE

When the blustery
Autumn breezes blow,
Up in the air
Kites and Piglet go!

L

IS

FOR

LADDER

A ladder is helpful
Going up and down trees,
When hunting for honey
Or running from bees.

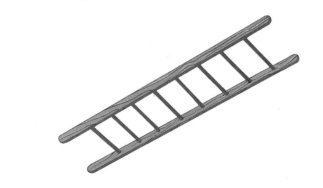

M

IS

FOR

MIRROR

"The Pooh in the mirror's
Quite clever," says Pooh.
"He knows how to copy
Whatever I do."

N

IS

FOR

NOSE

Why have we,
Do you suppose,
Two eyes, two ears,
But just one nose?

O

IS

FOR

OWL

Owl likes to talk a lot.
He's really quite a bore!
He tells Pooh everything he knows.
And sometimes even more!

P

IS

FOR

PIGLET

Piglet is so
Very small,
Sometimes he can't be
Seen at all!

Q

IS

FOR

QUILT

Let it snow and
Let it storm!
Under his quilt
Pooh is cozy and warm!

R

IS

FOR

RABBIT

Rabbit is so
Very busy.
Watching him
Makes Pooh Bear dizzy.

S

IS

FOR

SEESAW

Never make
A seesaw date
With a bear
Who's overweight!

T

IS
FOR
TIGGER

Though winter's here
And birds don't sing,
Tigger's tail still
Has its spring!

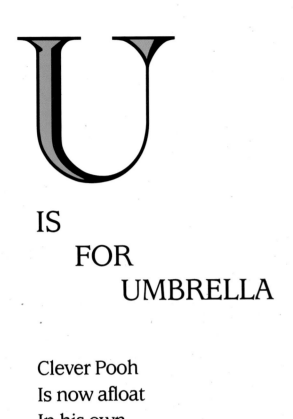

U

IS

FOR

UMBRELLA

Clever Pooh
Is now afloat
In his own
Umbrella boat!

V

IS

FOR

VEST

Piglet's vest
Is warm and snug.
It fits him like
An all-day hug!

W

IS

FOR

WOOZLE

There's nothing to fear
From a woozle it seems.
They're only found
In Pooh Bear's dreams.

X

IS
FOR
XYLOPHONE

Pooh's made a honey-pot
Xylophone,
And, oh, it has the
Sweetest tone.

Y

IS

FOR

YAWN

Put on your nightcap,
You old sleepyhead!
A yawn is what your face does
To say, "It's time for bed!"

Z

IS

FOR

ZZZZ

A sound that Pooh
Makes frequently
Begins and ends
With the letter Z.

ZZZZZZZ